All By Myself

written by Pam Holden
illustrated by Philip Webb

Dad said, "Let me help you sail your boat."

"No, I want to sail it
all by myself," said Tom.

"I could help you build your hut," said Dad.

"Please let me build it all by myself," said Tom.

"Let me help you feed your rabbit," said Dad.

"No, I want to feed him all by myself," said Tom.

"I could help you
hit the ball," said Dad.

"Please let me hit it
all by myself," said Tom.

"Let me help you catch a fish," said Dad.

"No, I want to catch one all by myself," said Tom.

"I could help you
ride your bike," said Dad.

"Please let me ride it
all by myself," said Tom.

"Let me help you
fly your kite," said Dad.

"No, I want to fly it all by myself," said Tom.

"Could you help me, Dad?"
shouted Tom.
"I want some help! Help!"